11/05   16.89

W9-BDC-817

An I Can Read Book™

Minnie and Moo
The Case of the Missing Jelly Donut

Denys Cazet

HarperCollins*Publishers*

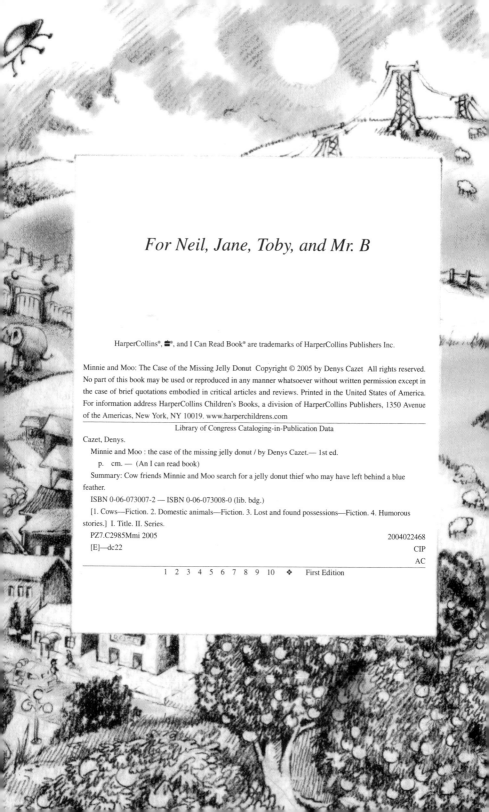

For Neil, Jane, Toby, and Mr. B

Minnie and Moo: The Case of the Missing Jelly Donut Copyright © 2005 by Denys Cazet All rights reserved.
No part of this book may be used or reproduced in any manner whatsoever without written permission except in
the case of brief quotations embodied in critical articles and reviews. Printed in the United States of America.
For information address HarperCollins Children's Books, a division of HarperCollins Publishers, 1350 Avenue
of the Americas, New York, NY 10019. www.harperchildrens.com
Library of Congress Cataloging-in-Publication Data
Cazet, Denys.
    Minnie and Moo : the case of the missing jelly donut / by Denys Cazet.— 1st ed.
        p.   cm. — (An I can read book)
    Summary: Cow friends Minnie and Moo search for a jelly donut thief who may have left behind a blue
feather.
    ISBN 0-06-073007-2 — ISBN 0-06-073008-0 (lib. bdg.)
    [1. Cows—Fiction. 2. Domestic animals—Fiction. 3. Lost and found possessions—Fiction. 4. Humorous
stories.] I. Title. II. Series.
    PZ7.C2985Mmi 2005   2004022468
    [E]—dc22   CIP
                                                                                                 AC
             1   2   3   4   5   6   7   8   9   10   ❖   First Edition

524-3257

The Stolen Donut

Minnie and Moo sat in the shade

of the old oak tree on the hill.

"Hey!" said Minnie. "It's gone!"

Moo put her book down.

"What's gone?" Moo asked.

"My jelly donut," said Minnie.

"I just took it out of the box."

"I put the box back and sat down," said Minnie. "Now the donut's gone!"

"Hmmm," muttered Moo. "I see."

"What do you see?" Minnie asked.

"I see a crime," said Moo.

"Your jelly donut was stolen!"

"Stolen!" said Minnie.

"Who would steal a jelly donut?"

"Evil knows no bounds!" said Moo.

She picked up a book called

Famous Farm Crimes of the Century.

"It's all in here," she said.

Moo showed Minnie a picture
of a duck robbing a feed store
in Kansas.

"Oh, my!" cried Minnie.

"It's so sad when a duck goes bad."

Moo picked up a blue feather.

"AHA!" she cried.

"The thief must have dropped this!

This feather is a clue.

Birds have feathers!

Chickens are birds!

The thief must be a chicken!"

"A chicken!" said Minnie.

"Yes!" said Moo. "A blue chicken!"

The Plan

Minnie followed Moo into the barn.

"Moo, what are you doing?"

"Solving the crime!" said Moo.

"When we find the blue chicken,

we'll find the stolen jelly donut!"

"But, Moo," said Minnie. "What if

the blue chicken ate the jelly—"

"Shhh," whispered Moo.

"The walls have ears.

Somewhere in this barn the thief

could be listening, watching,

waiting to strike again."

"Oh, my," said Minnie.

"Wasn't one jelly donut enough?"

"One is never enough," said Moo,

"for those who shop

in the supermarket of crime."

13

"Moo," said Minnie. "I—"

"I have a plan," whispered Moo.

"We dress up as chickens

and tonight, when they're asleep,

we search the chicken coop!"

"Moo, aren't we a little big to—"

"Minnie, who's going to notice two

more chickens in a henhouse?"

The New Chickens

Moo opened an old trunk.

"Try these on," she said.

Minnie and Moo dressed quickly.

"That looks good," said Moo.

"We'll use these funnels for beaks."

"What about those red things

on top of their heads?" asked Minnie.

15

"Use these rubber gloves," said Moo.

"They're extra large."

"Moo," said Minnie. "I feel silly.

It was just a jelly donut."

"Minnie, that donut was stolen.

Stealing is a crime.

What happens when the thrill
of stealing jelly donuts is gone?
What's next?
Candy from babies?
Tires from the school bus?
The farmer's false teeth
from his nightstand?"

"I don't know," said Minnie.

"What *is* next?"

"Pastries," said Moo. "Tarts, pies, birthday cakes, chocolate things!"

"What!" Minnie gasped.

"Why that dirty, stinking chicken!"

Sleeping Chickens

The moon hung over the henhouse.

Two huge chickens

crept up to the chicken coop.

"Shhh," said Moo. "Peek in."

Minnie turned on the flashlight.

She peeked into the coop.

"What do you see?" asked Moo.

19

"Sleeping chickens," said Minnie.

"What color?" asked Moo.

"Brown," said Minnie,

"and some white ones."

"Any blue ones?" Moo asked.

"No," said Minnie.

Moo peeked in.

"I see some empty roosts," she said.

"Maybe the blue chicken is out

robbing a feed store," said Minnie.

They heard a noise.

"What's that?" whispered Moo.

"Someone's coming," said Minnie.

"There! Coming down the road!"

A dark shape weaved its way

toward the chicken coop.

5

Giant Chickens

Elvis, the rooster, stopped

and hung on to a fence post.

"What a great party," he said.

"I know I was supposed

to count eggs tonight,

but if I can just sneak into the coop

without the chickens seeing me. . . ."

Elvis froze.

Two giant chickens stood
in front of the henhouse door.

"Geez Louize!" he gasped.

"Talk about extra-wide poultry!"

Minnie shined the light on Elvis.

"Hey!" said Elvis. "It wasn't me!"

"I wasn't at Little Willie's party!"

"He's not blue," said Moo.

"Right!" said Elvis. "I'm not blue.

I am feeling a little green.

But I am NOT blue, and I was NOT
at Little Willie's great party."

Minnie and Moo followed Elvis
into the henhouse.

Elvis sat on the edge of his bed.

He stared at the giant chickens.

"Man, those chickens are ugly,"

he muttered. "Still . . . I can't wait

to see the size of those eggs!"

The Blue Chicken?

Minnie and Moo sat in the coop.

The front steps creaked,

and the coop door opened slowly.

A dark figure slipped into the room.

"Is that the blue chicken?"

Minnie whispered.

"It's a fox," said Moo softly.

"Maybe the fox took your donut,"
said Moo.
"You mean the fox
is the blue chicken?" said Minnie.
"Shhh," whispered Moo.

Just as the fox started to slip a sack over Elvis, the rooster woke up. "Hey!" said Elvis.

"Quiet," said the fox. "I don't like chicken-leg dinners that talk."

Elvis showed the fox his leg.

"You call that dinner?" he said.

"I'll show you dinner."

Elvis pointed at Minnie's leg.

"Now THAT'S dinner!" he said.

"Wow!" said the fox.

Suddenly Minnie grabbed the fox.

"Did you steal my jelly donut?"

"NO! NO!" cried the fox. "HELP!"

"FOX!" shouted the chickens.

The fox scrambled out the door.

"And don't come back!" yelled Elvis.

The chickens rushed over to Elvis.

"Our hero!" they cried.

The Red Fish

The sun began to rise in the east.

Moo looked at the blue feather.

"AHA!" she said.

"What now?" said Minnie.

"This is not a blue feather!"

said Moo. "It's a red fish."

"It looks like a feather," said Minnie.

"It is a feather," said Moo. "But

this kind of clue is called a red fish.

That means it is a false clue!

The thief left the blue feather

to make us believe it was a real clue.

The thief wanted to lead us

on a wild goose chase."

"Another bird gone bad!"

said Minnie.

"The thief wanted us off the hill,"

said Moo, "so the thief could return

and commit the real crime."

"But, Moo, what's there to steal?" Minnie said. "All that's left are my— CREAM PUFFS!" she shouted.

The Crime Is Solved

Minnie and Moo rushed up the hill.

Minnie ran to the icebox.

She threw open the door

and took out a pink box.

She opened it and looked in.

"Moo!" she said. "They're all here!"

"Hmmm," hmmmed Moo.

Minnie took out a cream puff.

She bent over and put the box back.

"AHA!" said Moo.

"I know who took your jelly donut!"

"Who?" said Minnie.

"You!" said Moo.

"Me?" said Minnie. "Moo!
Why would I take my own donut?"

"Turn around," said Moo.

"What?" said Minnie.

"Turn around!" said Moo.

Minnie turned around.

Moo peeled off the jelly donut

that was stuck to Minnie's bottom.

"You didn't mean to steal it,"
said Moo. "You sat on it!"

"Oh, my," said Minnie.

Minnie sat down.

"The Case of the Missing Jelly Donut
is closed," Moo said.

"Oh, no!" Minnie cried.

"What?" said Moo.

"My cream puff," said Minnie.

"It's gone!"

ER Cazet   16.89
Cazet, Denys
Minnie and Moo; THe Case Of The
Missing Jelly Donut.

7/23 - 103x/23